S0-DJC-596

This edition is published by special arrangement with North-South Books Inc.

Grateful acknowledgment is made to North-South Books Inc., New York, for permission to reprint *Arthur Sets Sail* by Libor Schaffer, illustrated by Agnès Mathieu. Originally published in Switzerland under the title *Erwin, das abenteuerlustige Erdferkel.*

Printed in Mexico

ISBN 0-15-302133-0

4 5 6 7 8 9 10 050 97 96 95

Arthur
Sets Sail

Written by Libor Schaffer
Translated by Rosemary Lanning
Illustrated by
Agnès Mathieu

HARCOURT BRACE & COMPANY
Orlando Atlanta Austin Boston San Francisco Chicago Dallas New York
Toronto London

The land of the aardvarks lay beyond a great ocean. It had wide open spaces and a few craggy mountains, and was always bright and sunny. The soil was soft, sandy, and rather dry, so the trees and bushes didn't grow very high, and there were few flowers. Even so, it was a beautiful country that was just right for the aardvarks who lived there.

The sandy soil was so easy to dig, the aardvarks could make deep holes in the ground and rest there, shaded from the burning midday sun. And besides, this soil provided the one and only food the aardvarks liked: ants. The soil was teeming with them.

Since they had everything they needed to make them happy, none of the aardvarks ever thought of leaving their land.

Except Arthur. Arthur loved adventures. He was the only aardvark to climb the highest mountain in the land, and the only one who dared to go into the caves. He was looking for treasure that his grandfathers might have hidden there, but he didn't find any.

And what was Arthur's latest plan? He was building himself a boat to sail across the ocean.

The other aardvarks just shook their heads when they heard about it. "Where are you going?" they asked.

"Nowhere in particular," replied Arthur. "I'll just go where the wind blows me."

Arthur loaded supplies for his journey: a box of ants and a barrel of water. Now he was ready to set off.

Day after day Arthur sailed across the great ocean in his little boat. It felt wonderful to be rocked by the waves and fanned by a fresh, salty sea breeze with nothing but clear water all around him.

One day Arthur was starting his midday meal when he saw land on the horizon.

Was it the land of the aardvarks? Had his wonderful journey come to an end? Or was it another country?

The wind blew him straight toward the land. Arthur could see that it was a green and brown country with forests, high mountains, and dark green meadows. This was certainly not the land of the aardvarks.

When Arthur finally reached the shore of the unknown land he was met by a crowd of strange-looking animals. The aardvark scarcely believed his eyes; he had never seen such peculiar creatures before, chubby pink animals with no hair and no necks, with floppy ears and round faces. The strangest thing about them was their tails. They weren't really tails at all, just small, fat, curly things. Arthur found it difficult not to laugh.

When Arthur climbed out of his boat and the strange animals had their first good look at him they giggled, waggled their floppy ears, and rolled their eyes.

"Did you ever see anything like it?" they cried. "Just look at the skinny monster!"

Arthur was startled. Were these rude, curly-tailed creatures talking about him?

"Just look at him!" they shrieked. "What a funny shape! That head! Those feet! Those ears! And just look at the tail! It'd make a wonderful skipping rope."

Arthur was very hurt. "What kind of place have I landed in?" he sighed.

"This is the land of the rosy-pink pigs," the creatures chorused. "And where do you come from?"

"The land of the aardvarks," said Arthur with pride.

"Aardvarks? Come on!" giggled the pigs. "Did you ever hear anything like it?"

Arthur's stay in this strange country was far from pleasant. The pigs laughed and made fun of him whenever they saw him digging a hole or eating ants.

"No wonder you're nothing but skin and bone if that's all you eat," they chortled.

Arthur didn't answer. These rosy-pink guzzlers, who loved rolling in mud, walked along with their snouts pressed to the ground and ate everything they came across, didn't even deserve an answer.

For the first time in his life Arthur regretted having set out on an adventure. If only he'd stayed at home in his bright, airy land with its craggy mountains and plentiful ants. Here people just laughed at him and were rude. He couldn't dig a hole or hunt for ants in peace.

After two days the aardvark had had enough of the land of the rosy-pink pigs.

"I'm leaving," he said. "You're too bad-mannered for my liking."

"Where are you going?" asked Rudolf, one of the pigs.

"Home, to my own country," replied Arthur crossly. "To the wonderful land of the aardvarks."

"Does everyone there look like you?"

"Of course."

"I don't believe you! You're making it up," grunted Rudolf.

"If you don't believe me you can come and see for yourself," said Arthur in a huffy voice.

Rudolf pricked up his floppy ears. "Would you really take me with you?"

"I'd be glad to," said Arthur. "My boat is big enough. But you must promise me one thing."

"What's that?"

"To stop laughing at me."

So Arthur the aardvark and Rudolf the rosy-pink pig set off together.

When, after several days, they reached the coast of aardvark land a crowd was there to meet them. Scarcely had Rudolf the rosy-pink pig climbed out of the boat than the aardvarks began to laugh.

"Look at him! What a fatty!" they tittered. "Look at his head! His skin! And just look at those feet! The tail – have you ever seen a tail like that?"

"Quiet!" hissed Arthur furiously. "It was bad enough when the rosy-pink pigs laughed at me. You don't have to be so stupid. This is Rudolf. He's a rosy-pink pig and looks just like all the other ones. You shouldn't be rude about the way he looks."

The aardvarks were very ashamed of themselves and stopped making fun of the pig at once.

Rudolf said, "We really did behave like idiots, didn't we? I promise you it will never happen again."

From that day on ships often sailed between the two countries. Sometimes an aardvark visited the rosy-pink pigs and sometimes a rosy-pink pig sailed over the ocean to see the aardvarks.

And none of them ever laughed at each other again.